Pokémon

Meet the Pokémon of Johto

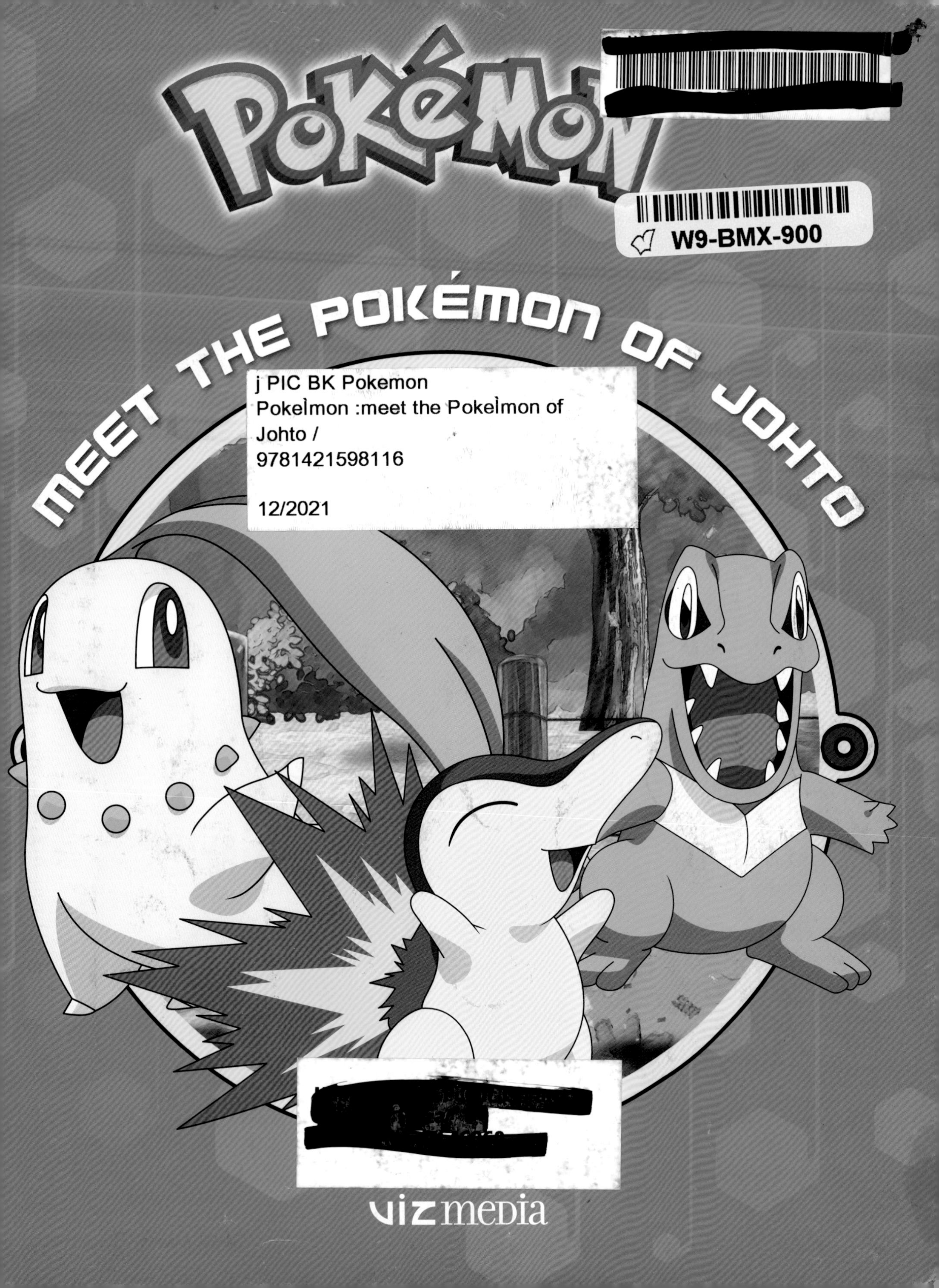

VIZ media

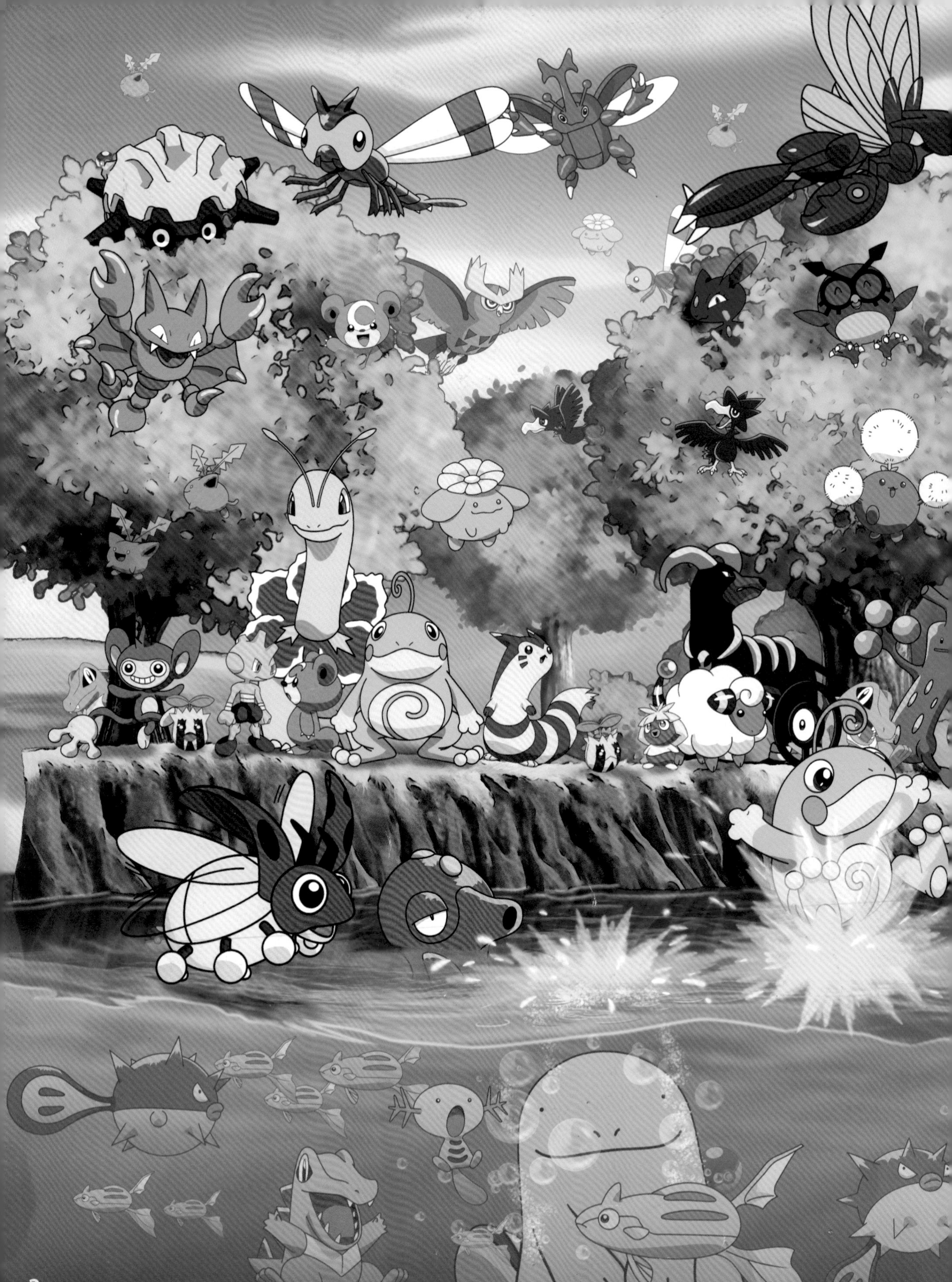

TOTAL EXCITEMENT

It's morning, and the Pokémon at the edge of the forest are all very excited. There's going to be a grand tournament in the afternoon, and everyone wants to participate. There's a festive atmosphere as the Pokémon play before the event begins.

LOOK FOR... ×6

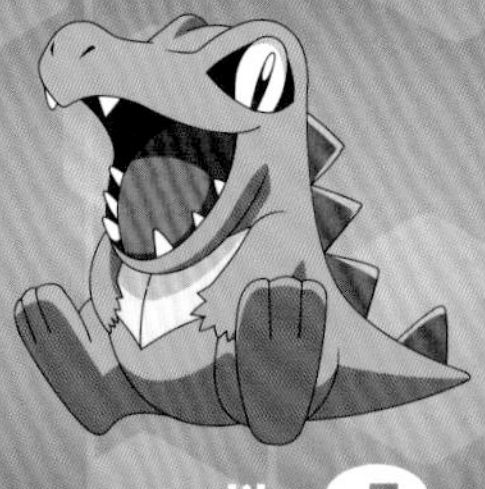

Totodile ×7

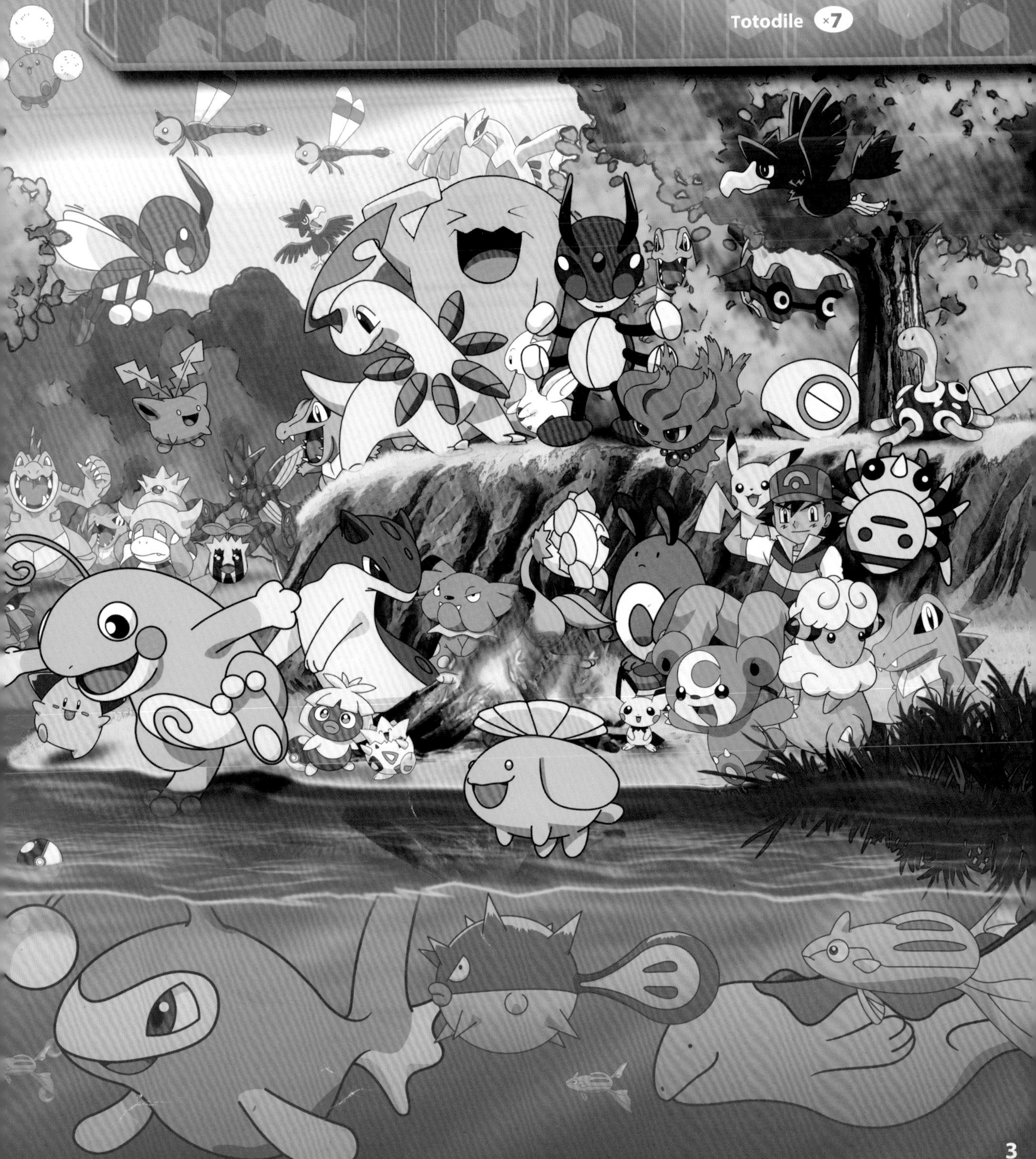

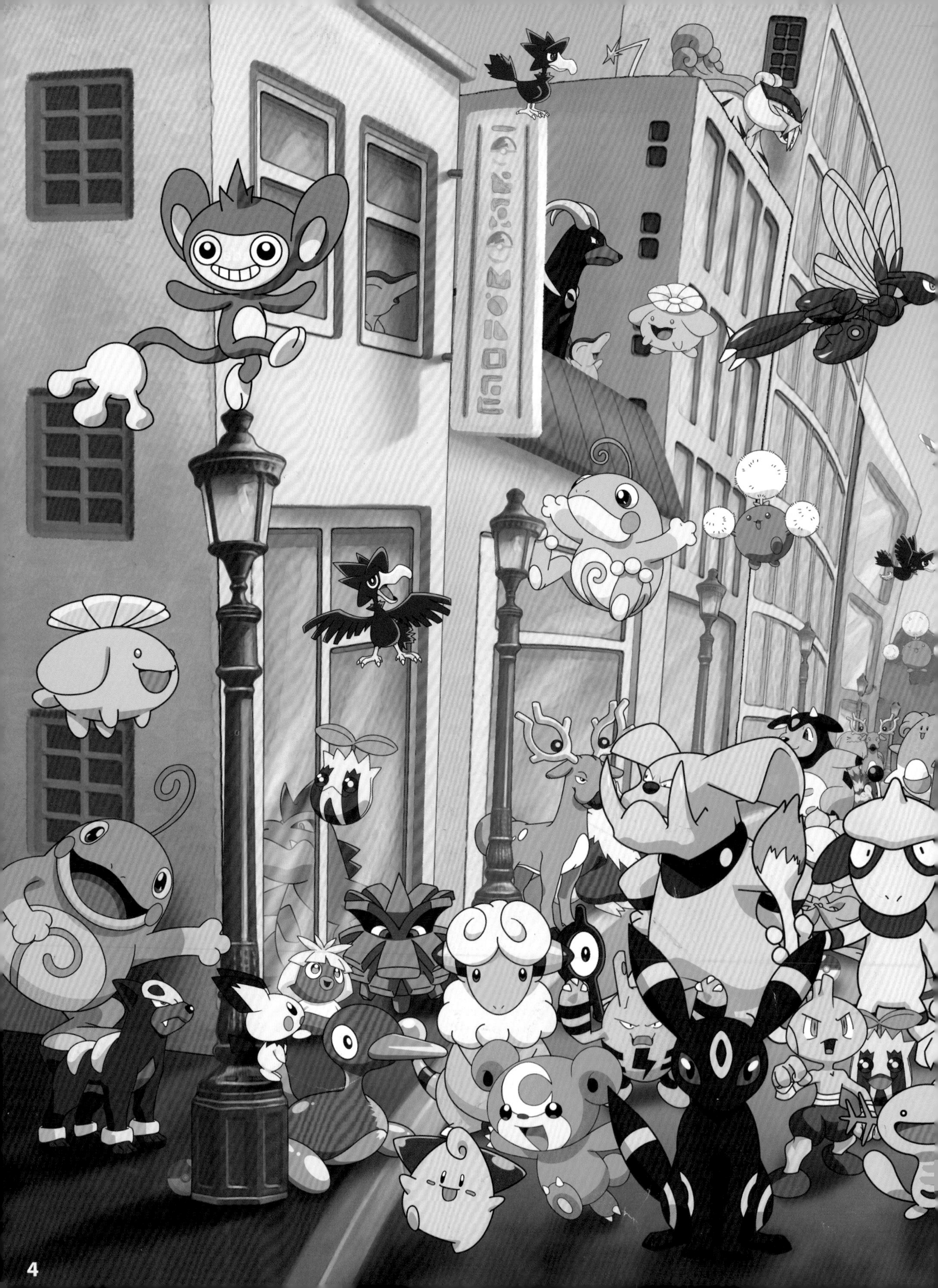

ARRIVING IN TOWN

The Trainers take their competitors to the Pokémon Center in the nearest town. They want to do some extra training to prepare for the tournament. But there are so many Pokémon already there! What a crowd! It would be so easy to get lost. As a matter of fact…where did Cyndaquil go?

LOOK FOR…

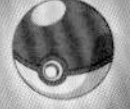
×3

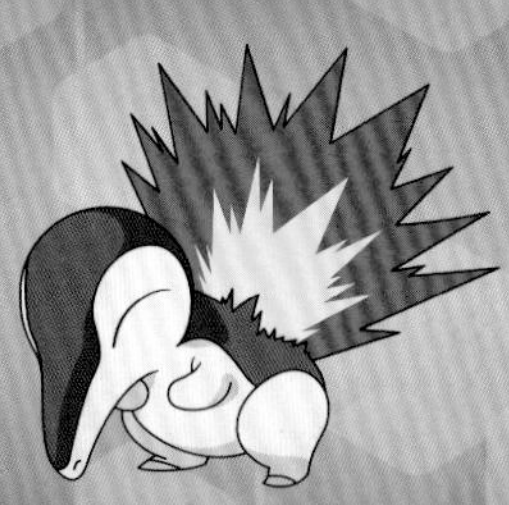

Cyndaquil ×6

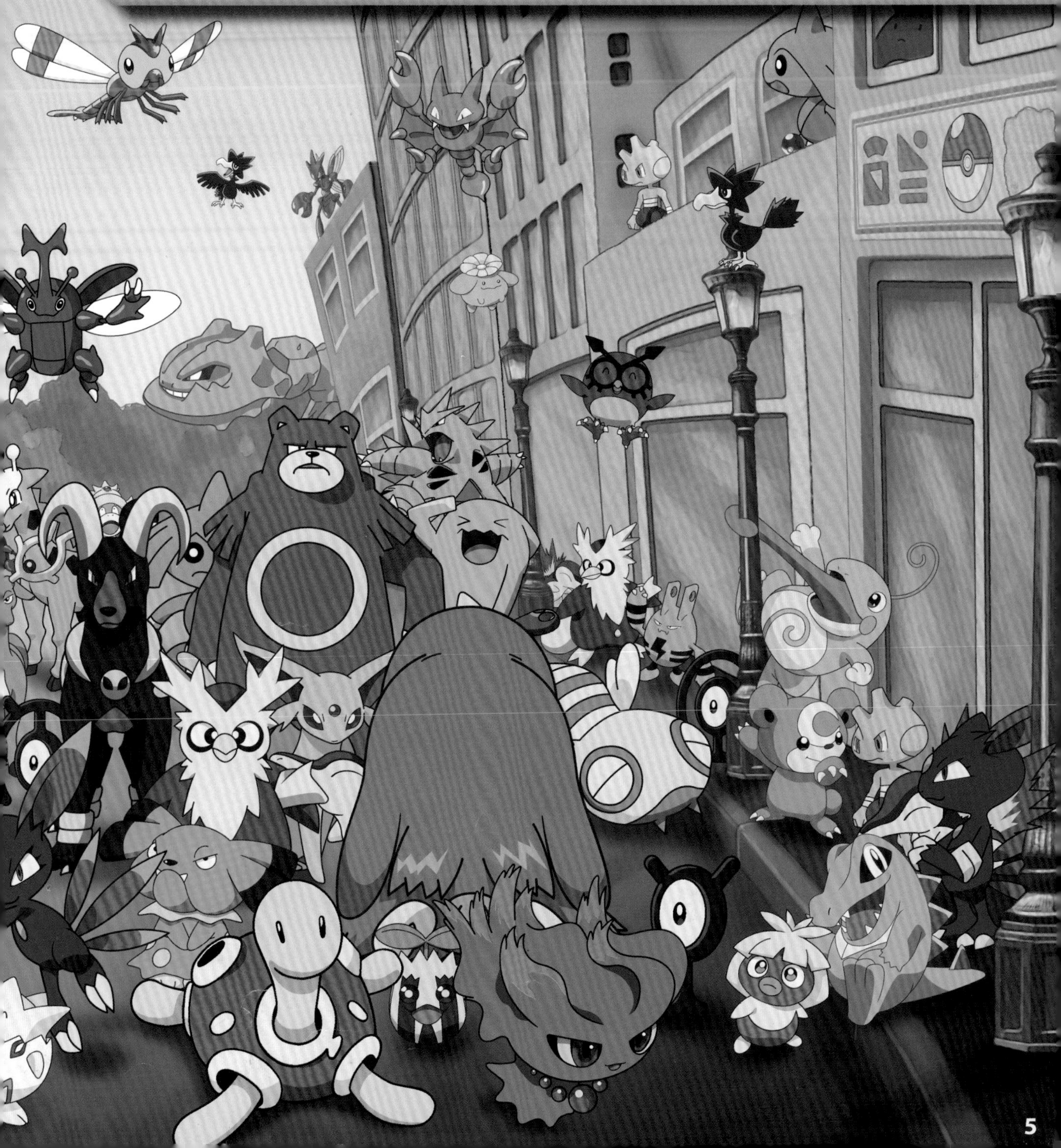

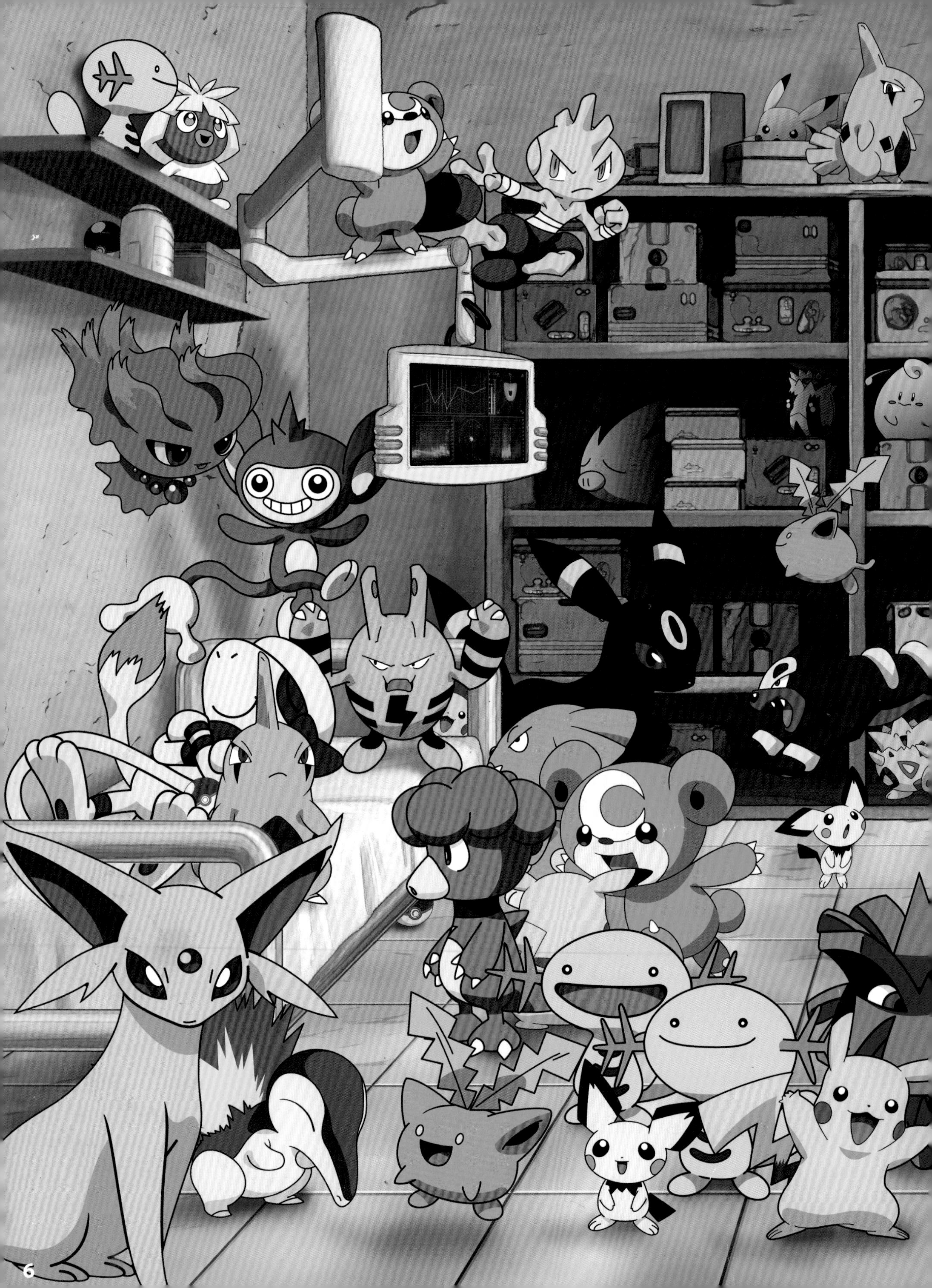

PANIC AT THE POKÉMON CENTER

Of course, it's just as busy at the Pokémon Center! The Trainers want their Pokémon to be in top shape, but it's impossible to keep them calm when they're all together like this. The second the Trainers glance away, the Pokémon disappear into the crowd. Where did Pikachu get to?!

LOOK FOR... ×6

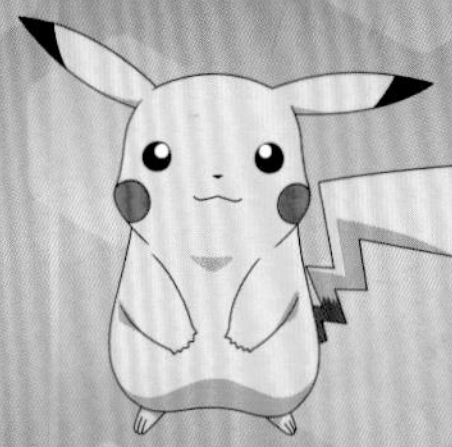

Pikachu ×6

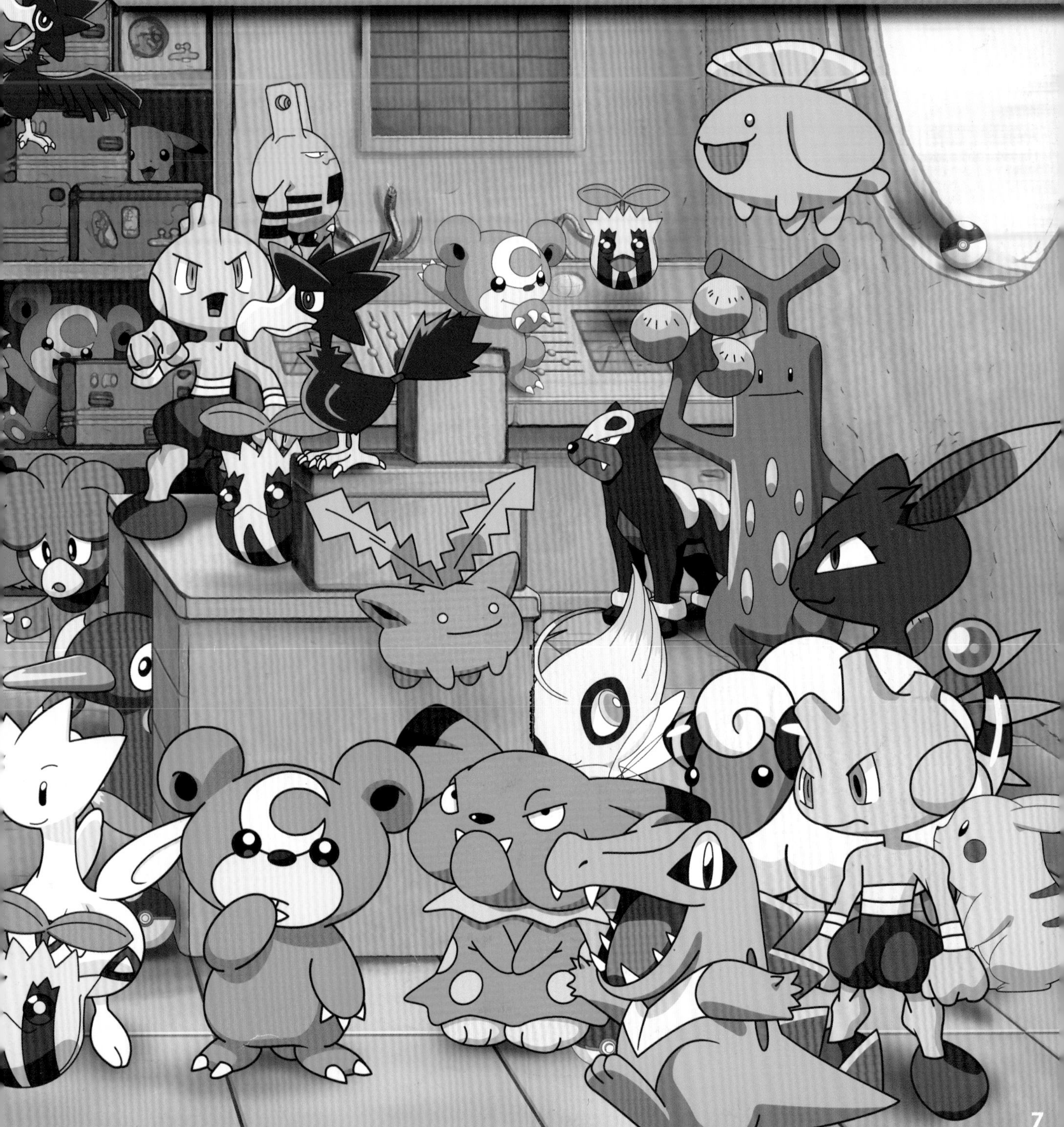

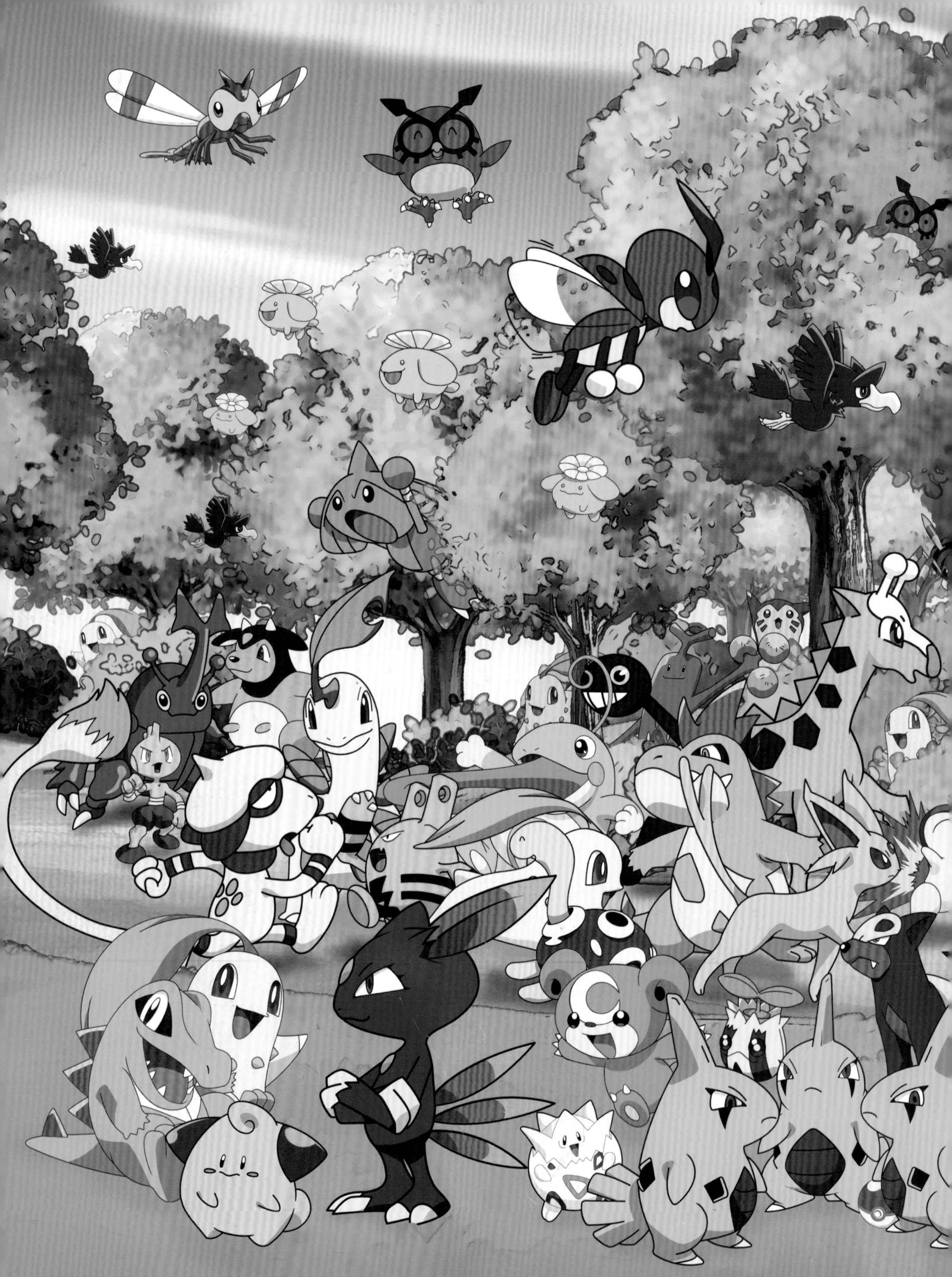

THE ROAD TO THE TOURNAMENT!

LOOK FOR... ×4

After a bit of a struggle, our friends are finally back on the road to the grand tournament. Johto is a magnificent region, and the forest they're traveling through is very beautiful. But the Pokémon are too busy making faces at each other to appreciate the scenery! In fact, it looks like we've lost a few Chikorita.

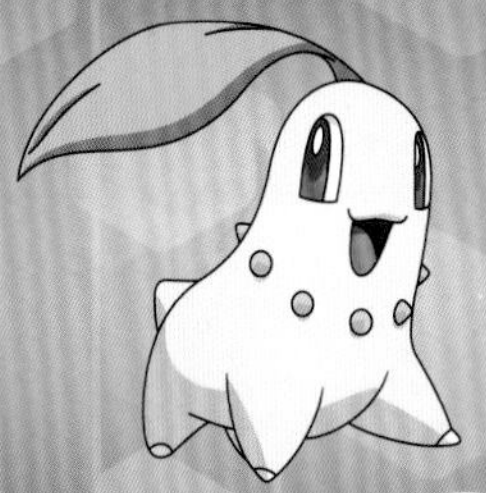

Chikorita ×6

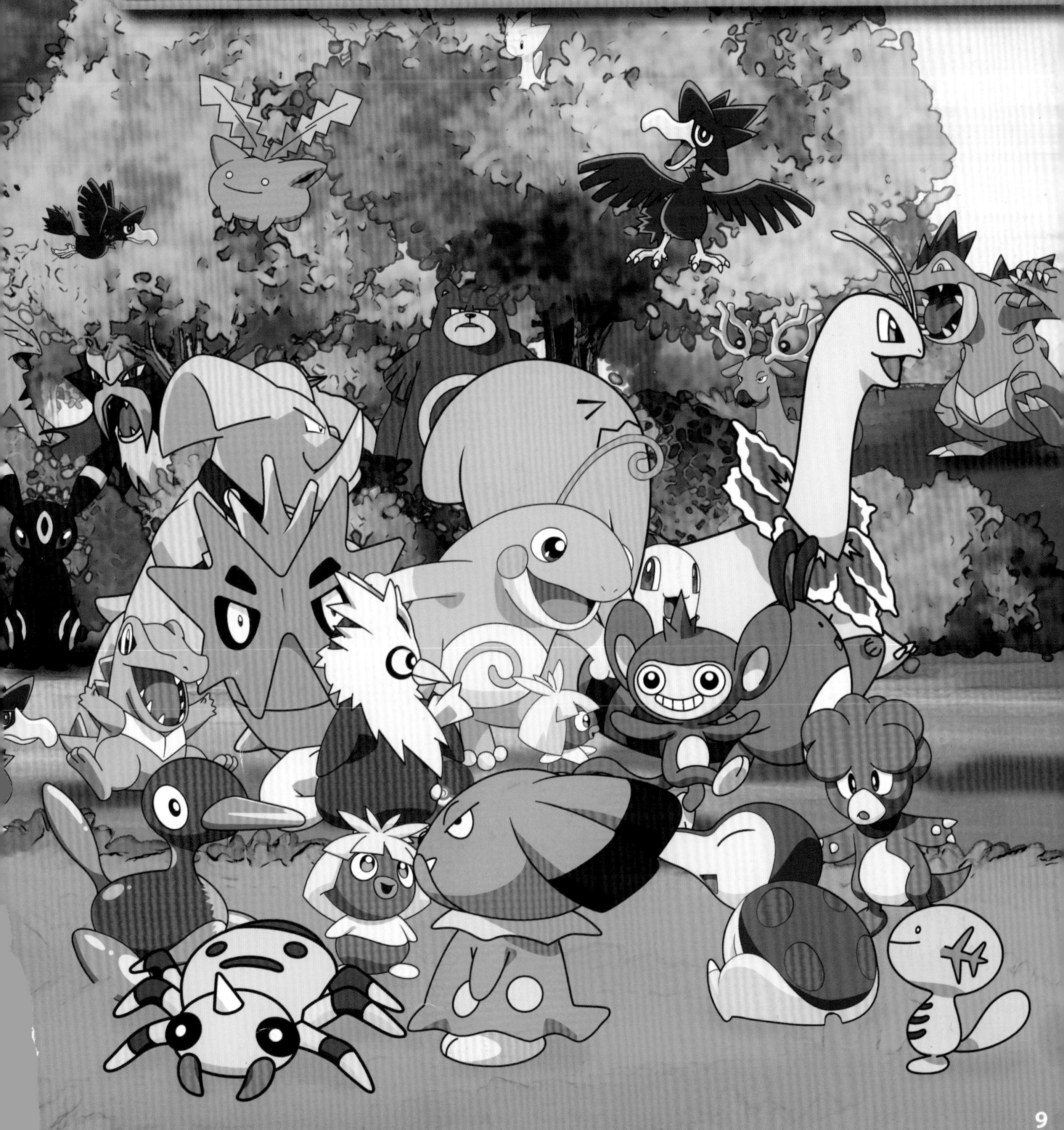

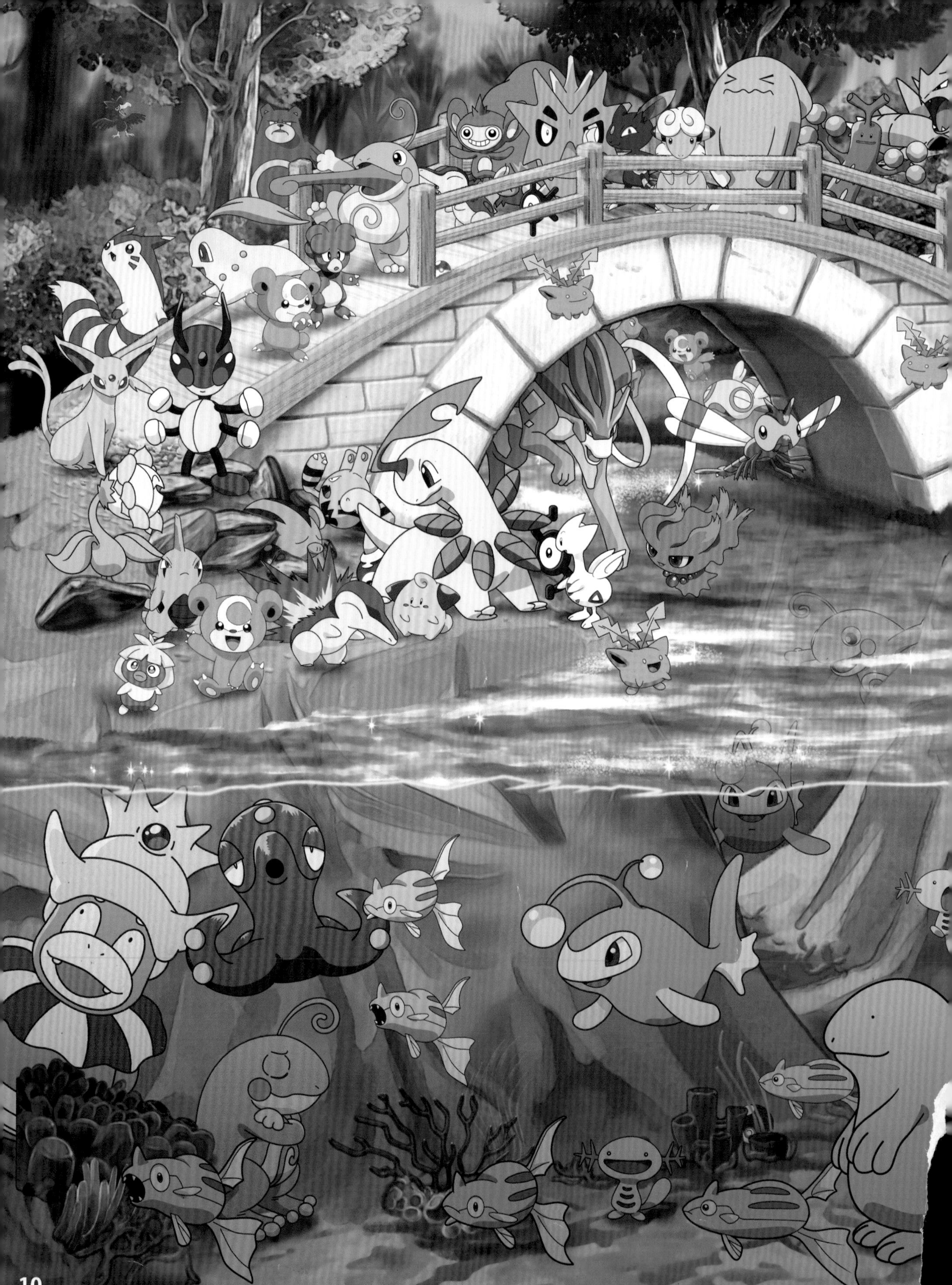

AQUATIC ENCOUNTERS

LOOK FOR... ×4

On their way to the tournament, our friends have an unexpected encounter. On the banks of a beautiful river, they get to meet aquatic Pokémon. Be careful not to lose sight of these Pokémon, who won't miss an opportunity to hide.

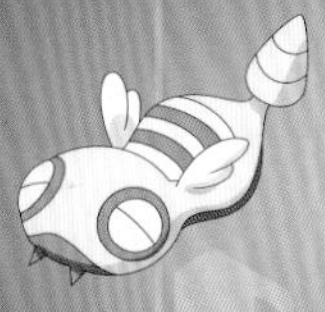

Dunsparce

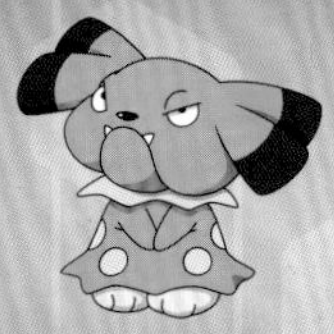

Snubbull

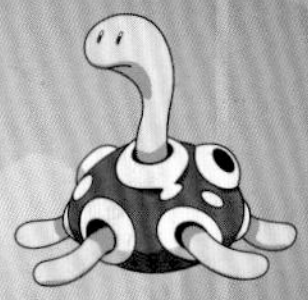

Shuckle

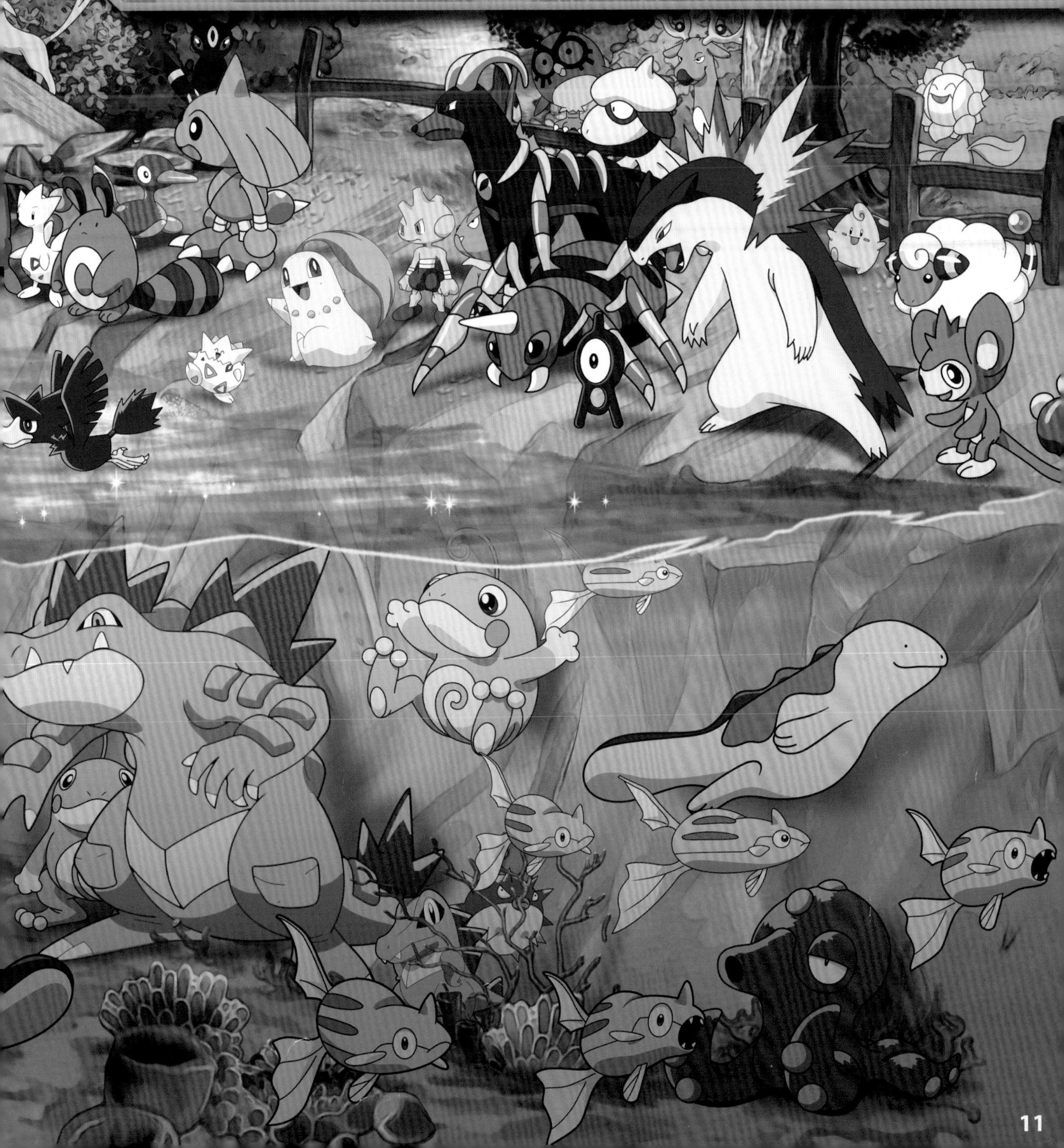

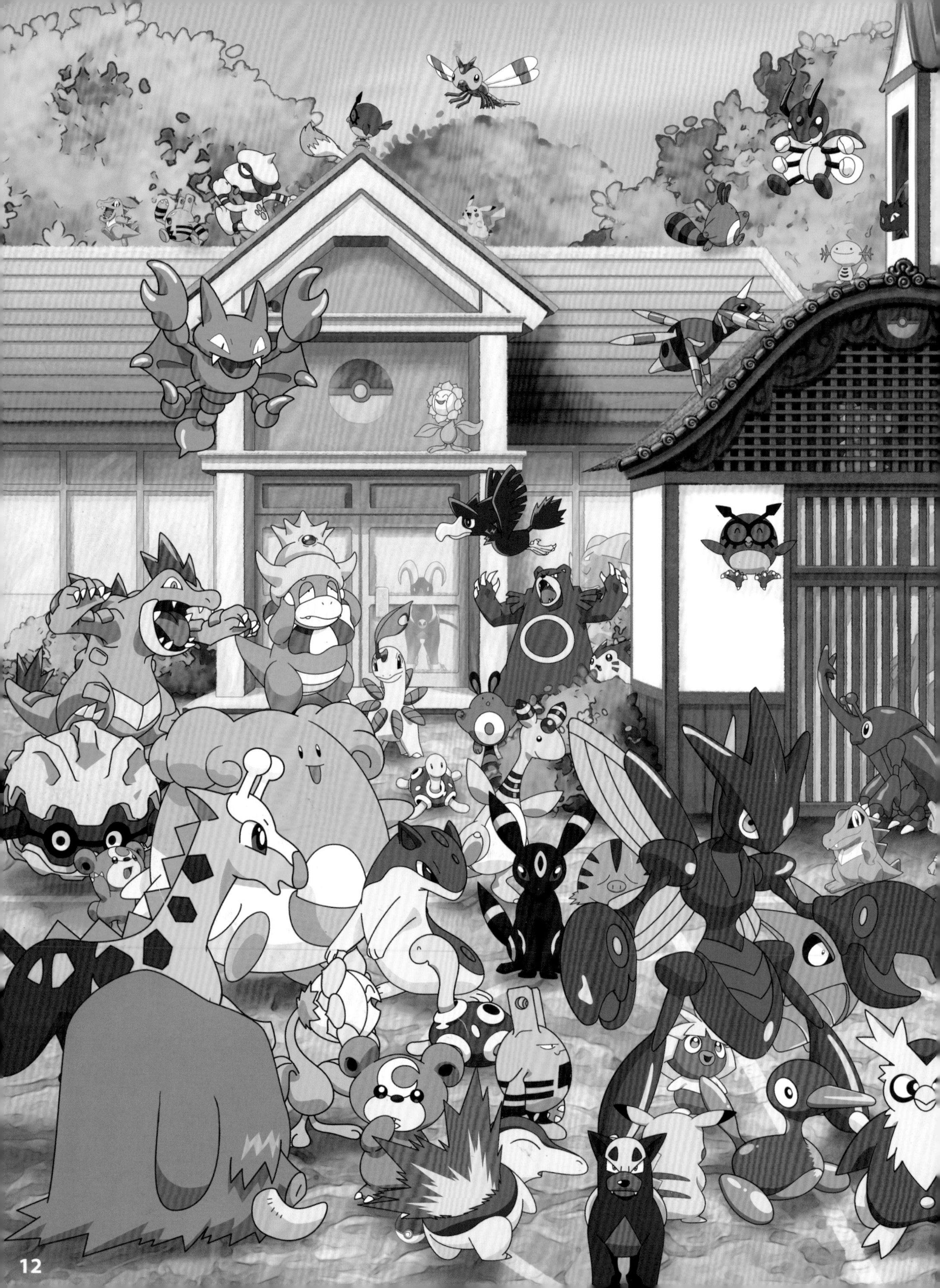

THE TENSION RISES

Our friends have arrived at their destination, and Ash is going to sign Pikachu up for the competition. Meanwhile, on the outer edge of the arena the atmosphere is electric, and it wouldn't take much to start a fight! Calm down, friends—save your energy for the tournament!

LOOK FOR... ×5

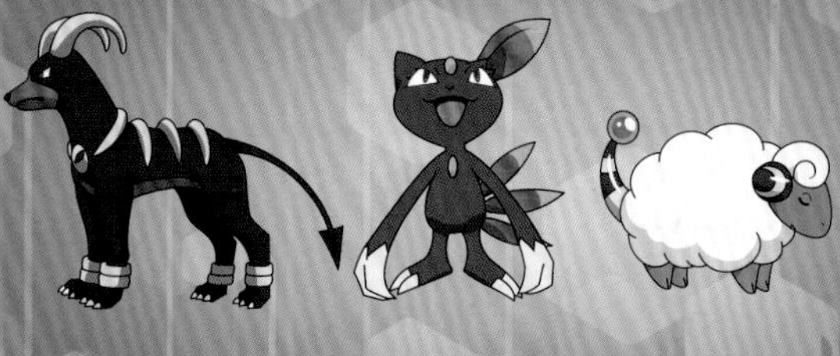

Houndoom Sneasel Mareep

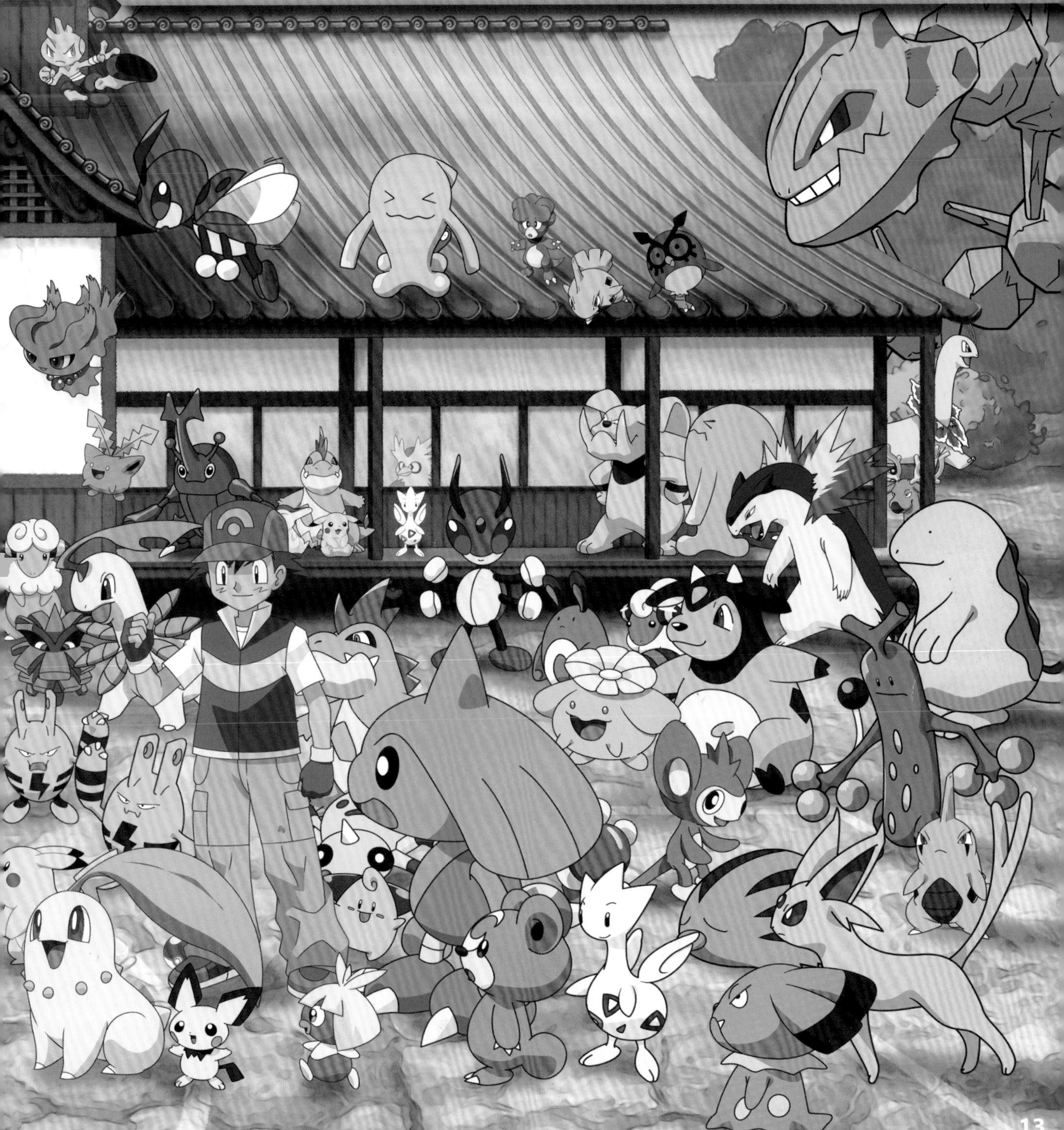

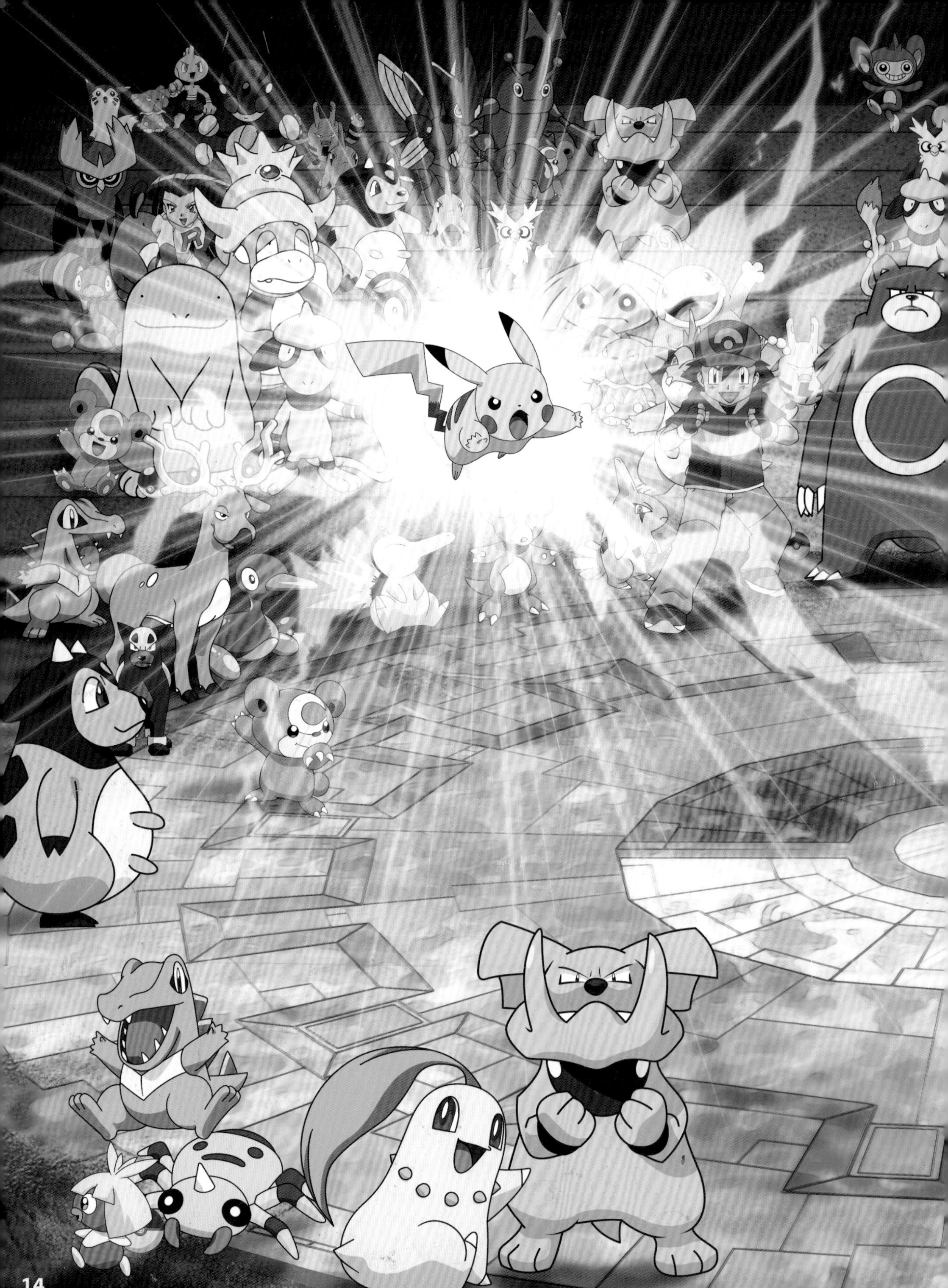

THE GRAND TOURNAMENT

What a spectacle! The battles take place one after another, each more intense than the last. The participants are all top-notch, and the winner will definitely be a true champion! And look, the Pokémon have attracted an envious audience…which means Team Rocket can't be far away. Keep your eyes open!

LOOK FOR... ×7

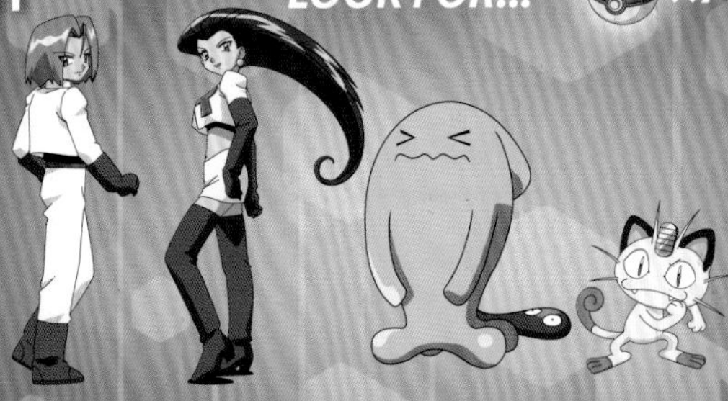

James Jessie Wobbuffet Meowth

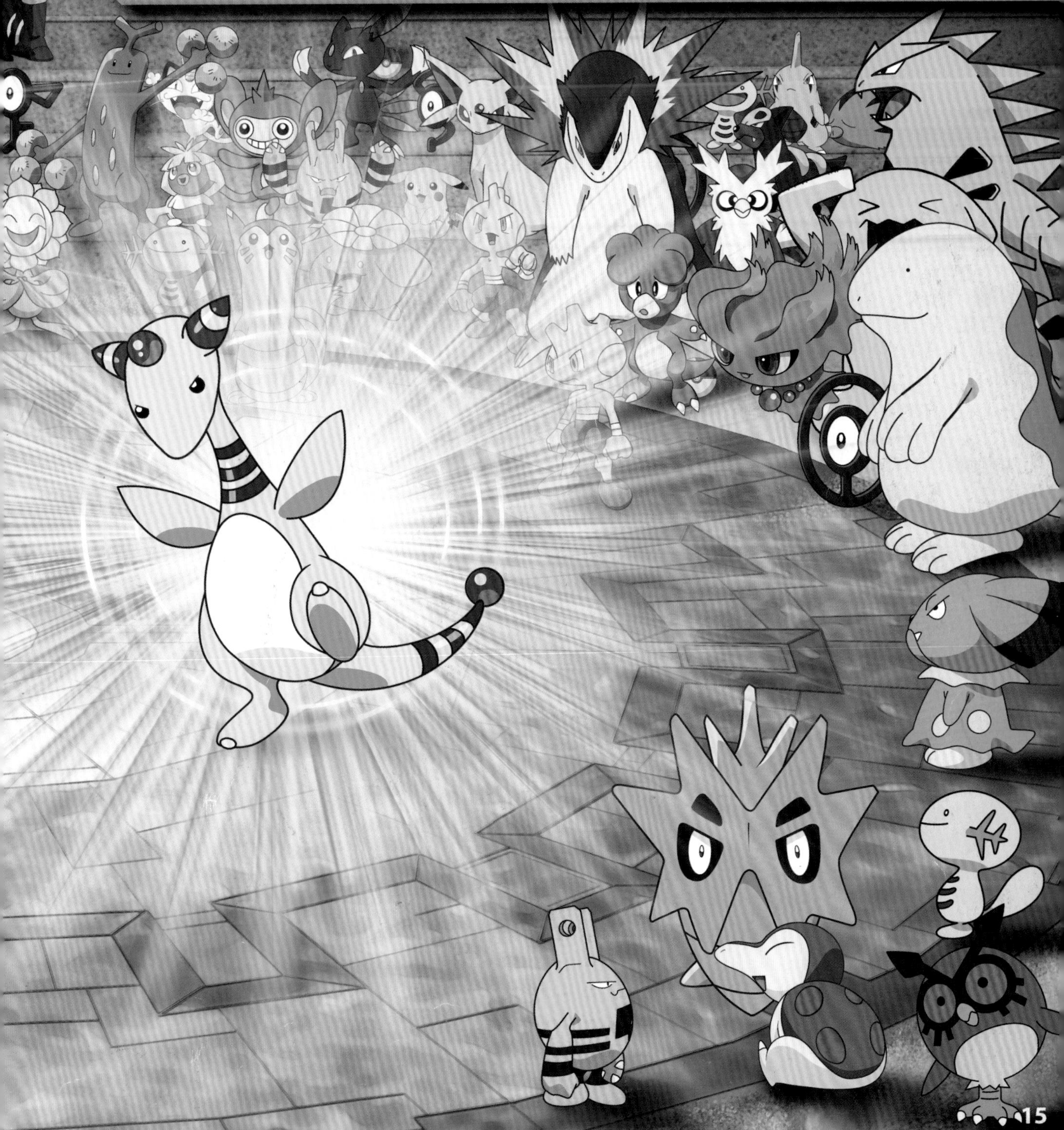

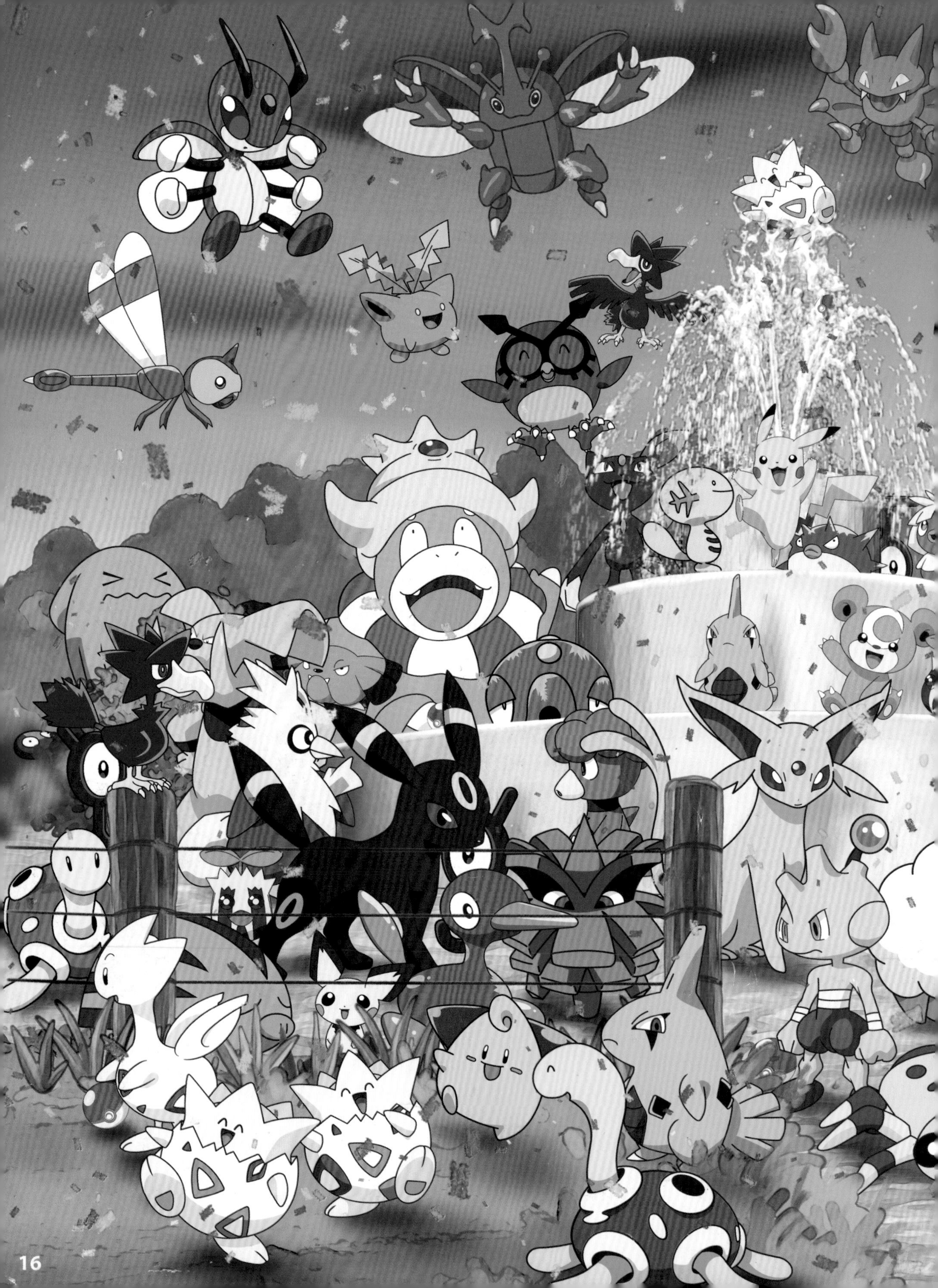

CHAMPION'S CELEBRATION

LOOK FOR... ×6

The tournament is over, and Ash is proud of his Pokémon—Pikachu's performance was breathtaking! Pikachu is carried in triumph to a celebratory party. Bravo, Pikachu! You deserve this victory! Some curious Unown have come to meet the new champion, too. Do you see them?

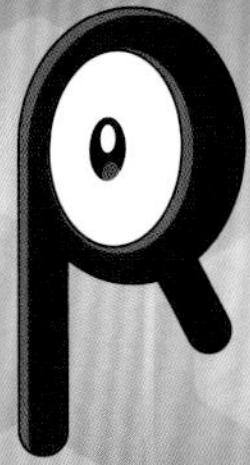

Unown ×6

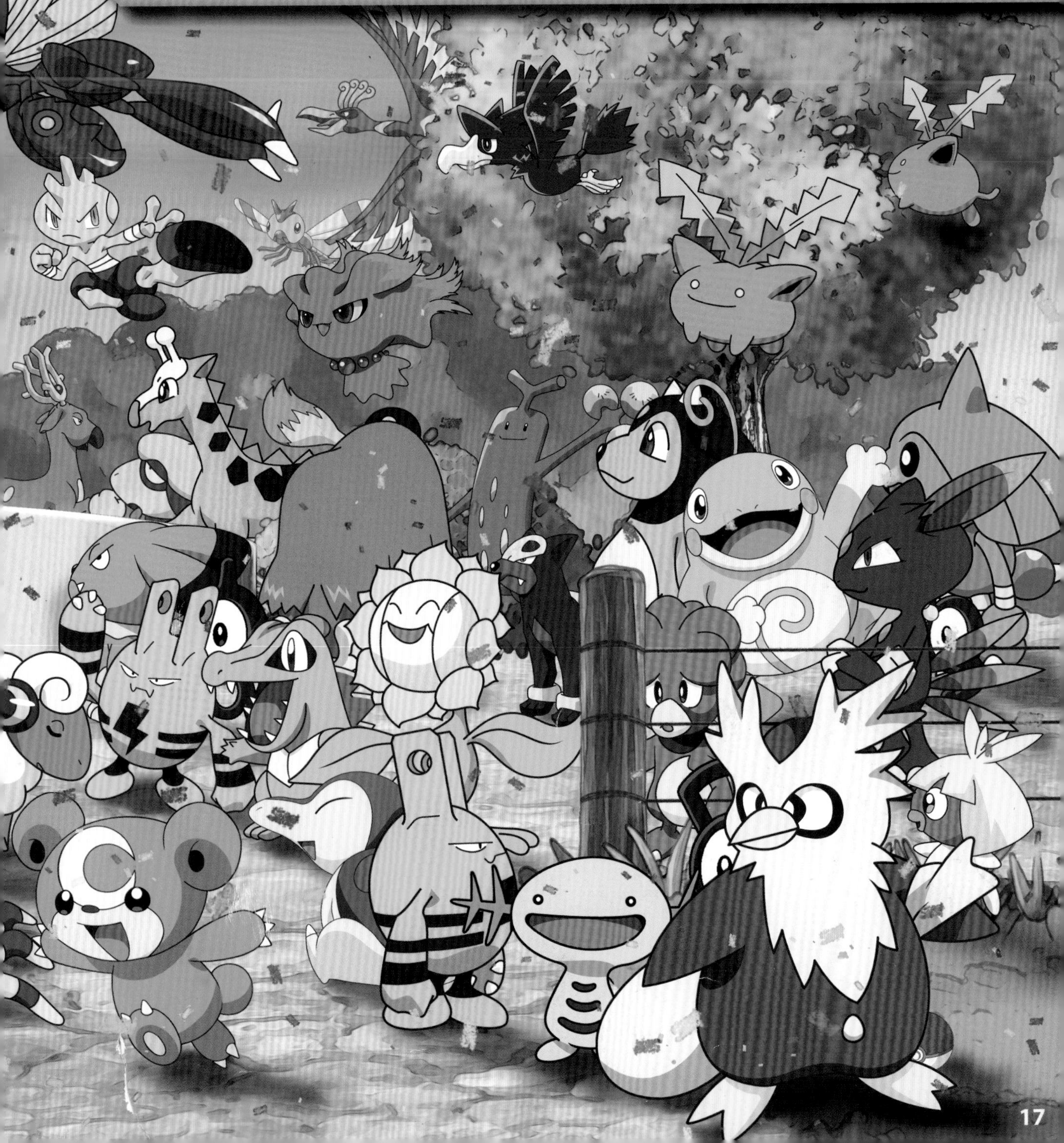

THE ULTIMATE CHALLENGE

Have you completed your mission and found all of the Pokémon in each of the scenes? If so, you're ready for the next challenge! Only the most exceptional Pokémon Trainers will succeed!

THE CHALLENGE OF THE LEGENDARY POKÉMON!

Suicune, Raikou, and Entei are hidden in the pages of this book.

YOU MUST FIND THEM!

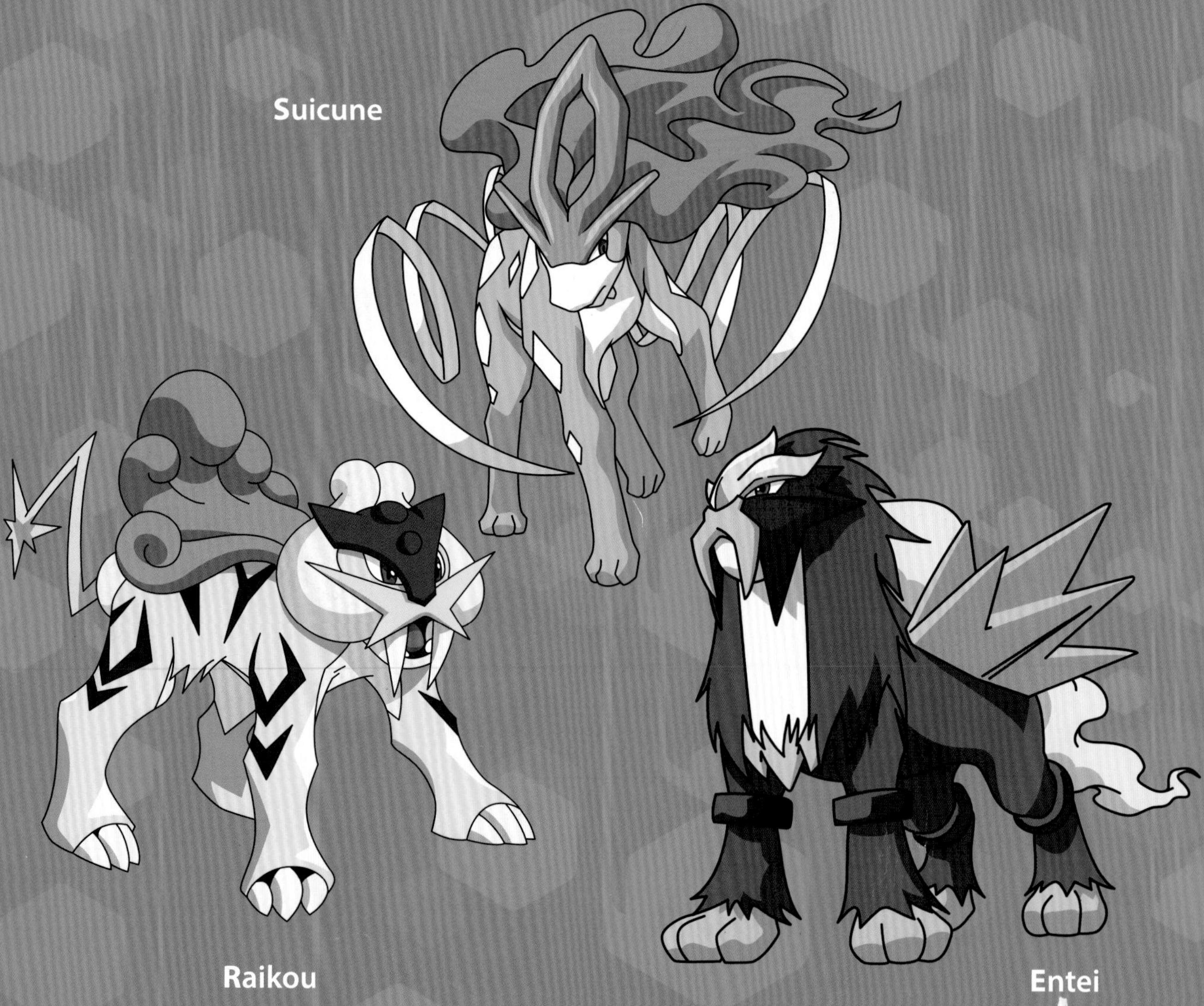
Suicune
Raikou
Entei

GUIDE TO THE POKÉMON OF JOHTO

CATEGORY:
BIG JAW POKÉMON
TYPE: WATER
HEIGHT: 7'07"
WEIGHT: 195.8 lbs
EVOLUTION:
Totodile ➤ Croconaw
➤ **Feraligatr**

FERALIGATR

Generally Feraligatr tends to move slowly, but when it spots prey it attacks with incredible speed.

WOOPER

By day, Wooper rests in the water to stay cool. At night, when the temperature drops, it goes out on the riverbank to hunt.

CATEGORY:
WATER FISH POKÉMON
TYPE: WATER-GROUND
HEIGHT: 1'04"
WEIGHT: 18.7 lbs
EVOLUTION:
Wooper ➤ Quagsire

CATEGORY:
AQUA RABBIT POKÉMON
TYPE: WATER-FAIRY
HEIGHT: 2'07"
WEIGHT: 62.8 lbs
EVOLUTION:
Azurill ➤ Marill ➤ **Azumarill**

AZUMARILL

With its long ears, Azumarill can detect the movements of Pokémon at the bottom of the river. The pattern on its belly serves as camouflage when it swims.

CATEGORY:
COTTONWEED POKÉMON
TYPE: GRASS-FLYING
HEIGHT: 2'07"
WEIGHT: 6.6 lbs
EVOLUTION:
Hoppip → Skiploom → **Jumpluff**

JUMPLUFF

When riding the wind, Jumpluff can steer itself with the cotton spores on its body and go anywhere the wind blows.

LEDYBA

Ledyba always group together—being alone fills them with doubt and makes them unable to move. When they get cold, they huddle together for warmth.

CATEGORY:
FIVE STAR POKÉMON
TYPE: BUG-FLYING
HEIGHT: 3'03"
WEIGHT: 23.8 lbs
EVOLUTION:
Ledyba → Ledian

CATEGORY:
FIVE STAR POKÉMON
TYPE: BUG-FLYING
HEIGHT: 4'07"
WEIGHT: 78.5 lbs
EVOLUTION:
Ledyba → **Ledian**

LEDIAN

The spot patterns on its back grow larger or smaller depending on the number of stars in the night sky. When the stars flicker, it flutters about, scattering a glowing powder.

CROCONAW

Croconaw has exactly 48 fangs in its mouth. If it loses one in the course of battle, a new one quickly grows back in its place.

CATEGORY:
BIG JAW POKÉMON
TYPE: WATER
HEIGHT: 3'07"
WEIGHT: 55.1 lbs
EVOLUTION:
Totodile → **Croconaw** → Feraligatr

HOUNDOOM

People used to believe Houndoom's bark was a bad omen. Its fiery breath causes incurable burns.

CATEGORY:
DARK POKÉMON
TYPE: DARK-FIRE
HEIGHT: 4'07"
WEIGHT: 77.2 lbs
EVOLUTION:
Houndour ➛ **Houndoom** ➛ Mega Houndoom

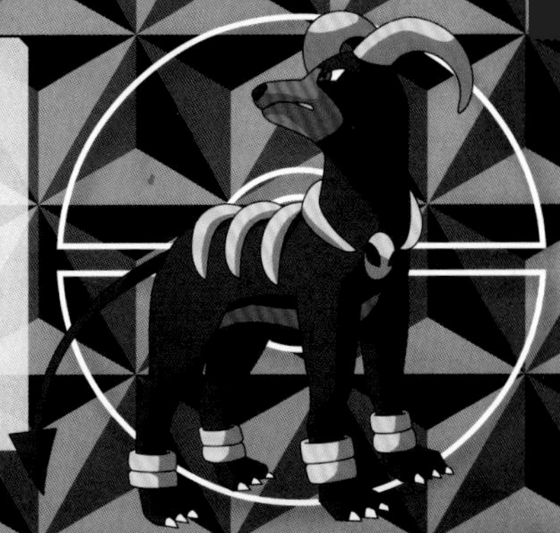

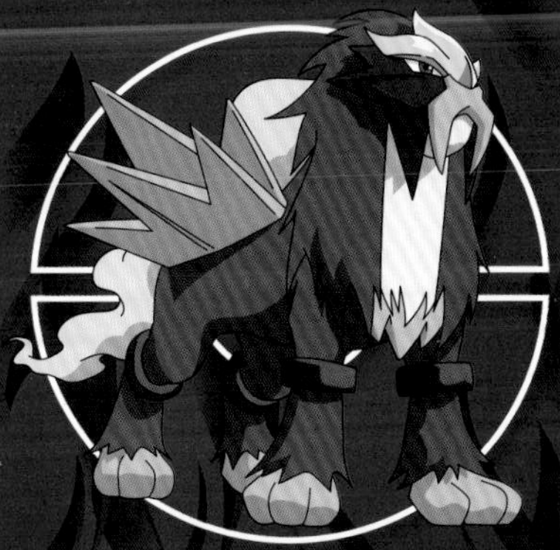

CATEGORY:
VOLCANO POKÉMON
TYPE: FIRE
HEIGHT: 6'11"
WEIGHT: 436.5 lbs
EVOLUTION:
This Pokémon does not evolve.

ENTEI

It's said that whenever Entei roars, it unleashes a volcanic eruption somewhere. It was born near a volcanic crater.

QUILAVA

When Quilava turns its back in the middle of combat, that doesn't mean it's throwing in the towel. It's steering its dorsal flames in the direction of its adversary.

CATEGORY:
VOLCANO POKÉMON
TYPE: FIRE
HEIGHT: 2'11"
WEIGHT: 41.9 lbs
EVOLUTION:
Cyndaquil ➛ **Quilava** ➛ Typhlosion

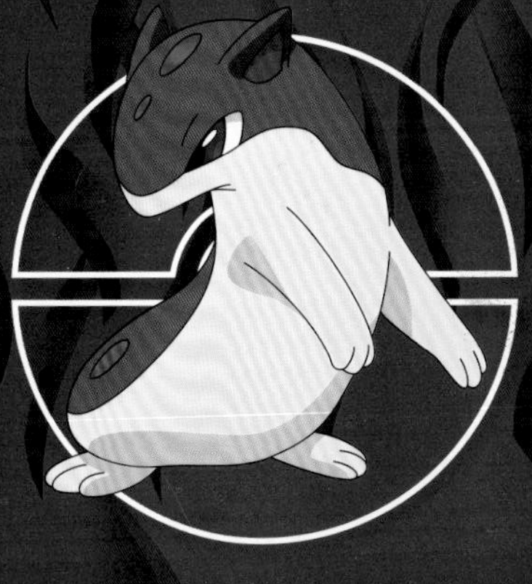

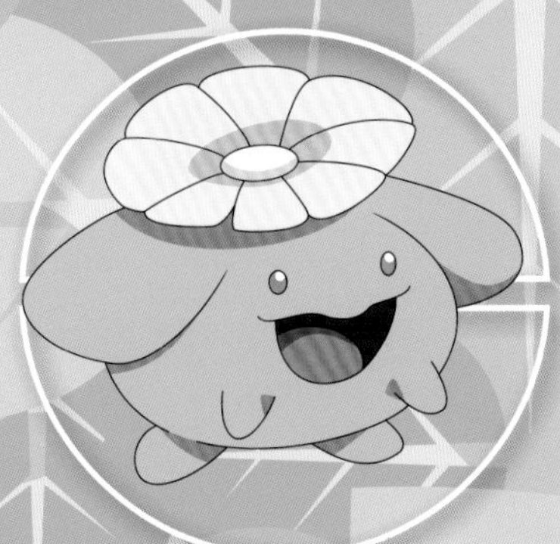

CATEGORY:
COTTONWEED POKÉMON
TYPE: GRASS-FLYING
HEIGHT: 2'00"
WEIGHT: 2.2 lbs
EVOLUTION:
Hoppip ➛ **Skiploom** ➛ Jumpluff

SKIPLOOM

Skiploom stretches its petals to absorb sunlight. Whether the flower on its head will bloom depends on the temperature: the flower closes when it's cold outside.

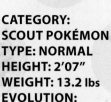

CATEGORY:
SCOUT POKÉMON
TYPE: NORMAL
HEIGHT: 2'07"
WEIGHT: 13.2 lbs
EVOLUTION:
Sentret ➜ Furret

SENTRET

Sentret is nervous by nature and is always alert. It stands on its tail to observe its surroundings and hits the ground with it to warn others when danger approaches.

CHIKORITA

Chikorita loves basking in the sun. Its leaf emits a pleasing aroma while gauging the humidity and temperature of the atmosphere.

CATEGORY:
LEAF POKÉMON
TYPE: GRASS
HEIGHT: 2'11"
WEIGHT: 14.1 lbs
EVOLUTION:
Chikorita ➜ Bayleef
➜ Meganium

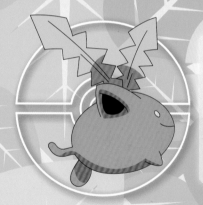

CATEGORY:
COTTONWEED POKÉMON
TYPE: GRASS-FLYING
HEIGHT: 1'04"
WEIGHT: 1.1 lbs
EVOLUTION:
Hoppip ➜ Skiploom ➜ Jumpluff

HOPPIP

Hoppip's body is so light it floats with the wind. It has to grip tightly with its feet to stay on the ground. If you see a group of them, it's a sure sign of the coming of spring.

CYNDAQUIL

Cyndaquil is shy and will roll up to protect itself. If something frightens or attacks it, its dorsal flame will flare up even more.

CATEGORY:
FIRE MOUSE POKÉMON
TYPE: FIRE
HEIGHT: 1'08"
WEIGHT: 17.4 lbs
EVOLUTION:
Cyndaquil ➜ Quilava
➜ Typhlosion

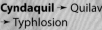

HO-OH

Legend has it Ho-Oh is seeking people of pure heart. In flight, its colorful, luminous wings create the appearance of a rainbow.

CATEGORY:
RAINBOW POKÉMON
TYPE: FIRE-FLYING
HEIGHT: 12'06"
WEIGHT: 438.7 lbs
EVOLUTION:
This Pokémon does not evolve.

CATEGORY:
DRAGON POKÉMON
TYPE: WATER-DRAGON
HEIGHT: 5'11"
WEIGHT: 335.1 lbs
EVOLUTION:
Horsea ➤ Seadra ➤ **Kingdra**

KINGDRA

Kingdra lives comfortably in the caverns at the bottom of the ocean. When it yawns, it swallows so much water it creates a whirlpool on the surface.

BELLOSSOM

When the rainy season ends, Bellossom dances while basking in the warm rays of the sun. The stinkier it was as Gloom, the more beautiful it will be as Bellossom.

CATEGORY:
FLOWER POKÉMON
TYPE: GRASS
HEIGHT: 1'04"
WEIGHT: 12.8 lbs
EVOLUTION:
Oddish ➤ Gloom ➤ Vileplume
or **Bellossom**

CATEGORY:
BIG JAW POKÉMON
TYPE: WATER
HEIGHT: 2'00"
WEIGHT: 20.9 lbs
EVOLUTION:
Totodile ➤ Croconaw
➤ Feraligatr

TOTODILE

Totodile is ferocious by nature, despite its small size. When surprised, it crushes everything that gets in the way of its terrible jaws.

CATEGORY:
LIGHT POKÉMON
TYPE: WATER-ELECTRIC
HEIGHT: 3'11"
WEIGHT: 49.6 lbs
EVOLUTION:
Chinchou ➜ **Lanturn**

LANTURN

Lanturn blinds its prey by shining a very bright light in their eyes, then swallows them whole while they are stunned. Because of the strength of its light, it's called the "Deep-Sea Star."

SMOOCHUM

When Smoochum finds something it's never seen before, it examines it with its sensitive lips. This Pokémon remembers everything it does and doesn't like.

CATEGORY:
KISS POKÉMON
TYPE: ICE-PSYCHIC
HEIGHT: 1'04"
WEIGHT: 13.2 lbs
EVOLUTION:
Smoochum ➜ Jynx

CATEGORY:
ANGLER POKÉMON
TYPE: WATER-ELECTRIC
HEIGHT: 1'08"
WEIGHT: 26.5 lbs
EVOLUTION:
Chinchou ➜ Lanturn

CHINCHOU

Chinchou live in the depths of the ocean, where they use their illuminated antennae to communicate with each other. They can also circulate electricity between their antennae.

LUGIA

Known as the guardian of the seas, Lugia sleeps in one of the faults in the deep-sea bed. According to legend, its wings can cause a hurricane lasting forty days.

CATEGORY:
DIVING POKÉMON
TYPE: PSYCHIC-FLYING
HEIGHT: 17'01"
WEIGHT: 476.2 lbs
EVOLUTION:
This Pokémon does not evolve.

BAYLEEF

The invigorating and spicy perfume of the buds that hang around the neck of Bayleef can make the people around it more energetic and healthy.

CATEGORY:
LEAF POKÉMON
TYPE: GRASS
HEIGHT: 3'11"
WEIGHT: 34.8 lbs
EVOLUTION:
Chikorita ➛ **Bayleef** ➛ Meganium

HOUNDOUR

If you hear a blood-chilling cry at dawn, it almost certainly means you've entered Houndour's territory.

CATEGORY:
DARK POKÉMON
TYPE: DARK-FIRE
HEIGHT: 2'00"
WEIGHT: 23.8 lbs
EVOLUTION:
Houndour ➛ Houndoom ➛ Mega Houndoom

QUAGSIRE

Quagsire lounges on river bottoms, waiting for prey. It's so easygoing that even if it bumps its head on rocks or boats while swimming it doesn't mind at all.

CATEGORY:
WATER FISH POKÉMON
TYPE: WATER-GROUND
HEIGHT: 4'07"
WEIGHT: 165.3 lbs
EVOLUTION:
Wooper ➛ **Quagsire**

MARILL

Marill has impenetrable fur that makes it possible for it to remain dry even when it's playing in water. Its tail functions as a buoy, which enables it to float easily.

CATEGORY:
AQUA MOUSE POKÉMON
TYPE: WATER-FAIRY
HEIGHT: 1'04"
WEIGHT: 18.7 lbs
EVOLUTION:
Azurill ➛ **Marill** ➛ Azumarill

CATEGORY:
HERB POKÉMON
TYPE: GRASS
HEIGHT: 5'11"
WEIGHT: 221.6 lbs
EVOLUTION:
Chikorita ➤ Bayleef ➤ **Meganium**

MEGANIUM

When Meganium breathes on dead flowers or dried herbs, they immediately come back to life. Its petals emit a calming perfume.

ESPEON

Espeon's incredibly sensitive fur means it can detect the smallest movements in the air. That's how it's able to detect meteorological shifts and predict what its adversaries will do.

CATEGORY:
SUN POKÉMON
TYPE: PSYCHIC
HEIGHT: 2'11"
WEIGHT: 58.4 lbs
EVOLUTION:
Eevee ➤ Vaporeon or Jolteon or Flareon or **Espeon** or Umbreon or Leafeon or Glaceon or Sylveon

CATEGORY:
MOONLIGHT POKÉMON
TYPE: DARK
HEIGHT: 3'03"
WEIGHT: 59.5 lbs
EVOLUTION:
Eevee ➤ Vaporeon or Jolteon or Flareon or Espeon or **Umbreon** or Leafeon or Glaceon or Sylveon

UMBREON

Umbreon's genetic structure is influenced by moonlight. When the moon is full, the rings on its body emit a faint glow.

PICHU

Pichu often play together by touching each other's tails and provoking electric shocks. They then lose control of their own electric charges, which causes unplanned bursts of electricity.

CATEGORY:
TINY MOUSE POKÉMON
TYPE: ELECTRIC
HEIGHT: 1'00"
WEIGHT: 4.4 lbs
EVOLUTION:
Pichu ➤ Pikachu ➤ Raichu

RAIKOU

It is said that when Raikou runs across the land, the rain clouds on its back shoot out bolts of lightning. Apparently, it arrived during a thunderstorm.

CATEGORY:
THUNDER
TYPE: ELECTRIC
HEIGHT: 6'03"
WEIGHT: 392.4 lbs
EVOLUTION:
This Pokémon does not evolve.

CATEGORY:
IMITATION POKÉMON
TYPE: ROCK
HEIGHT: 3'11"
WEIGHT: 83.8 lbs
EVOLUTION:
Bonsly → **Sudowoodo**

SUDOWOODO

Sudowoodo disguises itself as a tree in order to protect itself, but its bodily composition resembles a rock. It actually hates the open air and avoids the rain.

SUICUNE

Suicune has the ability to purify water. Whenever this Pokémon appears, the north wind blows.

CATEGORY:
AURORA POKÉMON
TYPE: WATER
HEIGHT: 6'07"
WEIGHT: 412.3 lbs
EVOLUTION:
This Pokémon does not evolve.

CATEGORY:
FROG POKÉMON
TYPE: WATER
HEIGHT: 3'07"
WEIGHT: 74.7 lbs
EVOLUTION:
Poliwag → Poliwhirl → Poliwrath or **Politoed**

POLITOED

When two or more Politoed get together, they begin to sing in a chorus.

TEDDIURSA

Teddiursa hides food everywhere it can to prepare for winter. Its paws are covered in honey, which means it always has something to nibble on.

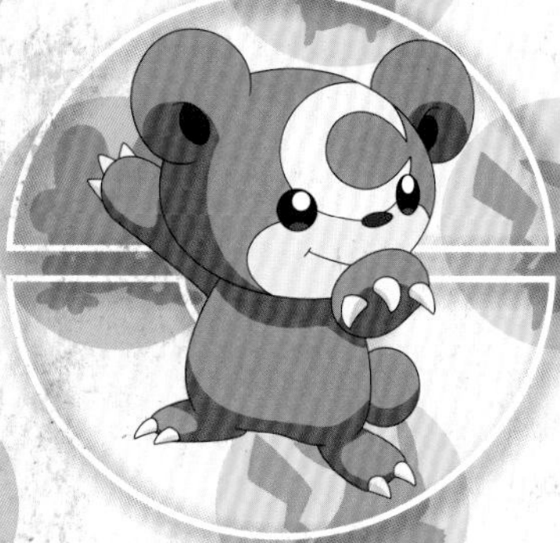

CATEGORY:
LITTLE BEAR POKÉMON
TYPE: NORMAL
HEIGHT: 2'00"
WEIGHT: 19.4 lbs
EVOLUTION:
Teddiursa ➛ Ursaring

IGGLYBUFF

Igglybuff has extremely small paws, which is why it usually bounces around instead of walking. When it feels threatened, it will start rolling and cannot stop.

CATEGORY:
BALLOON POKÉMON
TYPE: NORMAL-FAIRY
HEIGHT: 1'00"
WEIGHT: 2.2 lbs
EVOLUTION:
Igglybuff ➛ Jigglypuff ➛ Wigglytuff

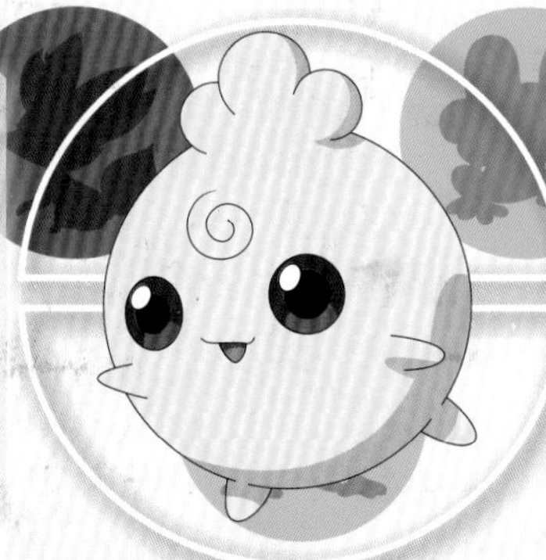

TYPHLOSION

When Typhlosion is angry, it becomes so hot that anything it touches goes up in flames. It can cause huge explosions with its burning fur.

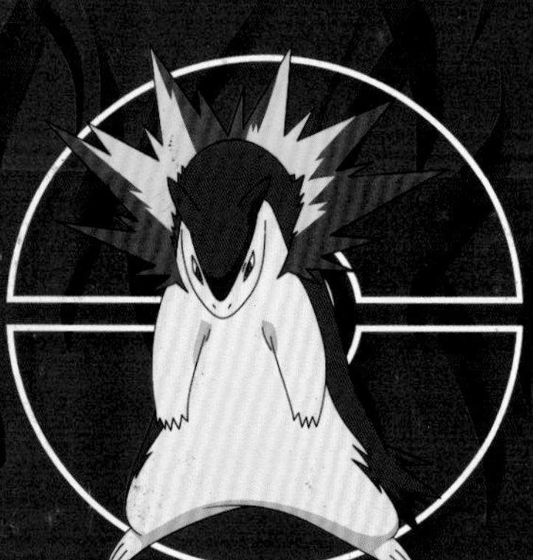

CATEGORY:
VOLCANO POKÉMON
TYPE: FIRE
HEIGHT: 5'07"
WEIGHT: 175.3 lbs
EVOLUTION:
Cyndaquil ➛ Quilava ➛ **Typhlosion**

URSARING

Ursaring climbs trees to find nourishment and sleep. Thanks to its very developed sense of smell, it always finds food buried underground.

CATEGORY:
HIBERNATOR POKÉMON
TYPE: NORMAL
HEIGHT: 5'11"
WEIGHT: 277.3 lbs
EVOLUTION:
Teddiursa ➛ **Ursaring**

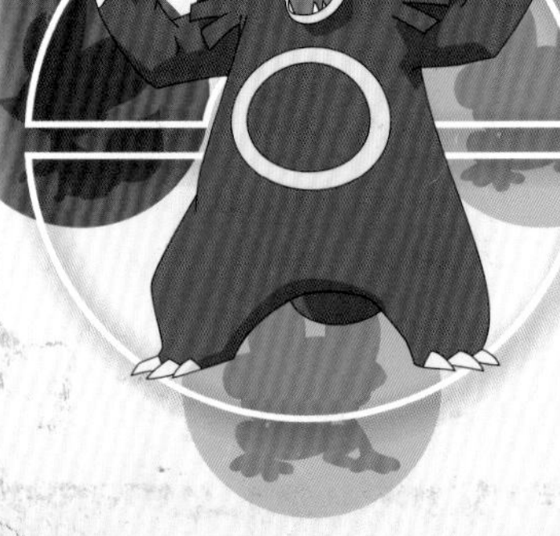